For my sister Sam and her 'tiger' Tallulah. x

Text and illustrations copyright © 2012 Rebecca Elliott
This edition copyright © 2012 Lion Hudson

The moral rights of the author
have been asserted

A Lion Children's Book
an imprint of
Lion Hudson plc
Wilkinson House, Jordan Hill Road,
Oxford OX2 8DR, England
www.lionhudson.com
Paperback ISBN 978 0 7459 6349 5
Hardback ISBN 978 0 7459 6384 6

First paperback edition 2012
1 3 5 7 9 10 8 6 4 2 0
First hardback edition 2012
1 3 5 7 9 10 8 6 4 2 0

A catalogue record for this book is available
from the British Library

Typeset in 23/28 Pink Martini OT
Printed in China May 2012 (manufacturer LH17)

Distributed by:
UK: Marston Book Services Ltd, PO Box 269, Abingdon, Oxon OX14 4YN
USA: Trafalgar Square Publishing, 814 N Franklin Street, Chicago, IL 60610
USA Christian Market: Kregel Publications, PO Box 2607, Grand Rapids, MI 49501

The Last TigeR

Rebecca Elliott

LION
CHILDREN'S

Luka lived in a strange world,
where the people had forgotten what was important.

There were no trees, no plants... and no animals.

Except one.
The last tiger.

One night the tiger's paw got caught in an old tin can.
Luka ran to see what the noise was.

A... TIGER?

He gently pulled the tiger's giant paw from the can.
The tiger **smiled,** and **nodded.**

And then he ran away.

"Wait!"

Luka followed the tiger until he disappeared
into his **dark** and **secret** cave.

Then the tiger emerged with a present
for Luka.

"Thank you!"

After that, they became

best friends.

But they only played together
when no one was looking.

Or so they thought...

One night, a giant net whooshed
the tiger up into the sky.

"No!"
cried Luka.

SHPLAM!

Luka tried to get near his friend
but the crowds were too big.

"The last tiger!"
the people shouted.

Luka felt lonely and scared.
He decided to hide in the tiger's secret cave.

To his **amazement**, inside the cave he found...

a beautiful garden!

Luka rushed back and pushed his way through the crowds.

"I know about your secret garden! I think
we should show them."

The tiger **smiled**, and **nodded**.
Luka turned to the crowd:

Luka and the tiger took the people through the cave door
and into the garden.

"Wow!"

Everyone remembered what the world once looked like and they longed to make it happen again.

"Please teach us!" they said to the tiger.

And the tiger **smiled**...

and nodded.